Tiny Fox and Great Boar

There

Written and Illustrated by Berenika Kołomycka
Lettered by Crank!

AN ONI PRESS PUBLICATION

Designed by Kate Z. Stone
Edited by Chris Cerasi, Sarah Gaydos, and Grace Scheipeter

Published by Oni-Lion Forge Publishing Group, LLC.

James Lucas Jones, president & publisher • Charlie Chu, e.v.p. of creative & business development • Steve Ellis, s.v.p. of games & operations • Alex Segura, s.v.p of marketing & sales • Michelle Nguyen, associate publisher • Brad Rooks, director of operations Amber O'Neill, special projects manager • Margot Wood, director of marketing & sales Katie Sainz, marketing manager • Henry Barajas, sales manager • Tara Lehmann, publicist • Holly Aitchison, consumer marketing manager • Troy Look, director of design & production • Angie Knowles, production manager • Kate Z. Stone, senior graphic designer • Carey Hall, graphic designer • Sarah Rockwell, graphic designer Hilary Thompson, graphic designer • Vincent Kukua, digital prepress technician Chris Cerasi, managing editor • Jasmine Amiri, senior editor • Shawna Gore, senior editor • Amanda Meadows, senior editor • Robert Meyers, senior editor, licensing Desiree Rodriguez, editor • Grace Scheipeter, editor • Zack Soto, editor • Ben Eisner, game developer • Jung Lee, logistics coordinator • Kuian Kellum, warehouse assistant

Joe Nozemack, publisher emeritus

1319 SE Martin Luther King Jr. Blvd.
Suite 240
Portland, OR 97214

onipress.com
f 🐦 📷 @onipress

@berenikamess
@ccrank

First Edition: March 2022
ISBN: 978-1-63715-020-7
eISBN: 978-1-63715-029-0

1 2 3 4 5 6 7 8 9 10

Library of Congress Control Number: 2021940871

Printed in China

Here

This is Tiny Fox.

This is his apple tree.

This valley is his home.

Tiny Fox was always alone, but he never felt sad. Like most small animals, he went about his day believing he was happy.

9

Everything was different now, under the apple tree.

Tiny Fox, so used to doing everything by himself, had to learn how to share.

He even had to share his favorite game of rolling downhill.

Soon, fall came to the valley.

Great Boar went on living beneath the apple tree.

bump

bump

Tiny Fox was not pleased with sharing his apples, but what could he do?

One afternoon, Tiny Fox took a walk in the woods near the apple tree.

Now and then, he'd look back to see if Great Boar was following him.

~phew~

hop

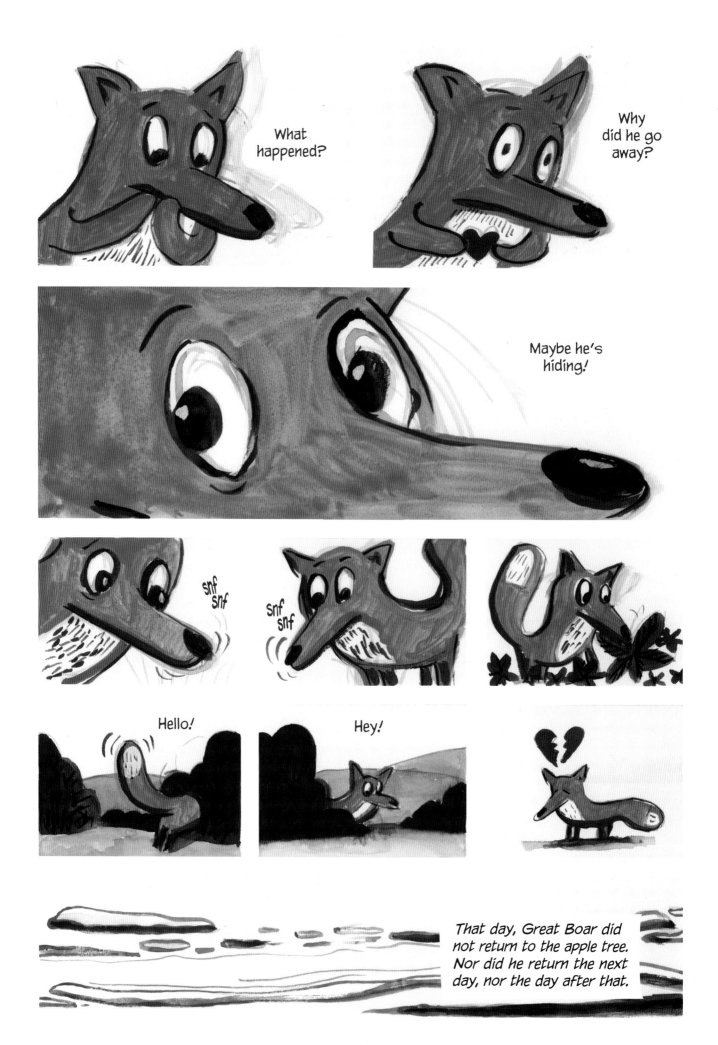

Great Boar had simply disappeared.

Days passed...

...and nights, too.

And still, Tiny Fox waited under the apple tree.

Together

Soon, fall passed them by.

The wind began to blow.

Winds that carried away the birds...

...and the leaves, too.

But those very same winds blew something new into the valley...

A scarf.

Soon, the winds stopped.

The scarf landed in the apple tree.

The same apple tree that was home to Tiny Fox and Great Boar!

A scarf.

It's beautiful.

How did it get here?

The winds brought it.

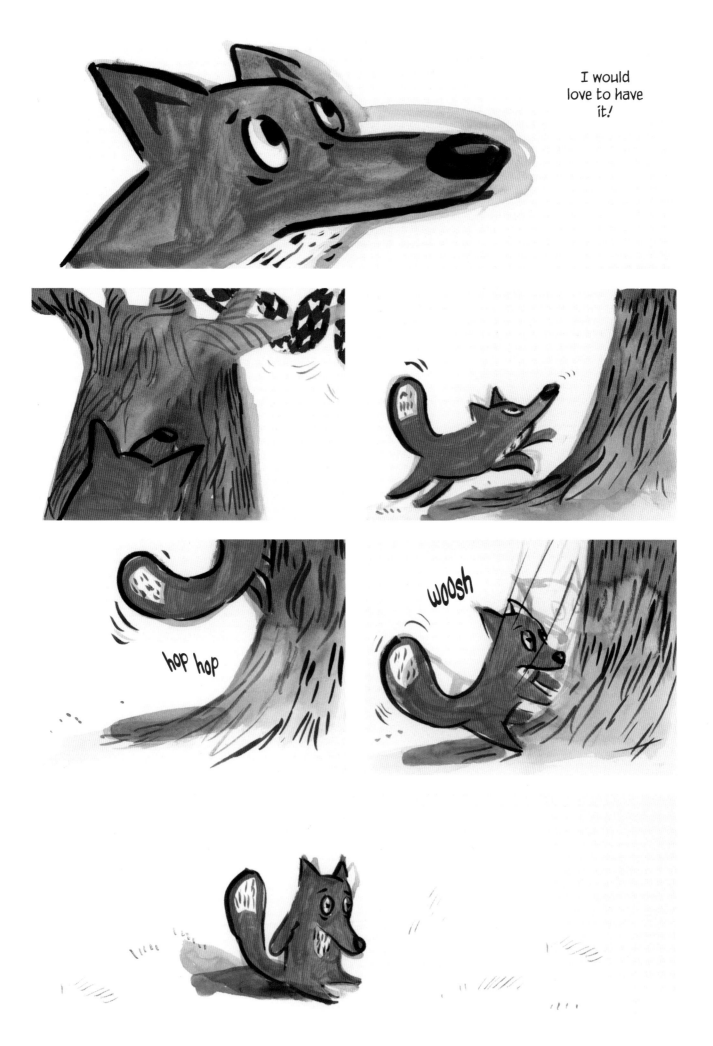

Don't worry, Tiny Fox. When the wind blows again, the scarf will fall.

But the wind didn't blow again.

And snow began to fall.

26

Apart

Winter had
certainly arrived.

The snow covered
the whole valley.

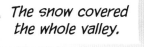

Tiny Fox and Great Boar
were freezing even with
their lovely scarves.

Time passed slowly
as they walked.

The cold was biting.

Their paws and
hooves were like
ice cubes, frozen
from the snow.

39

Acorns!

crunch
crunch

?!

Look!

And so, Tiny Fox and Great Boar figured out a **new** plan.

Because as we know by now...

...together is always better.

There

The two friends rowed and rowed their boat.

They slept upon the lake.

Perhaps they were dreaming about tomorrow, and the new adventures they would have.

The two friends
ran and ran.

They ran into
the woods...

...and climbed
through some
thickets.

It was hard work, but they
were excited about the nice
things they might find.

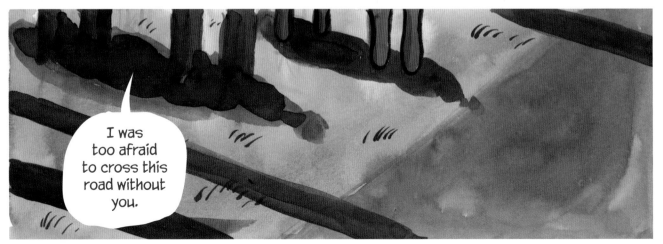

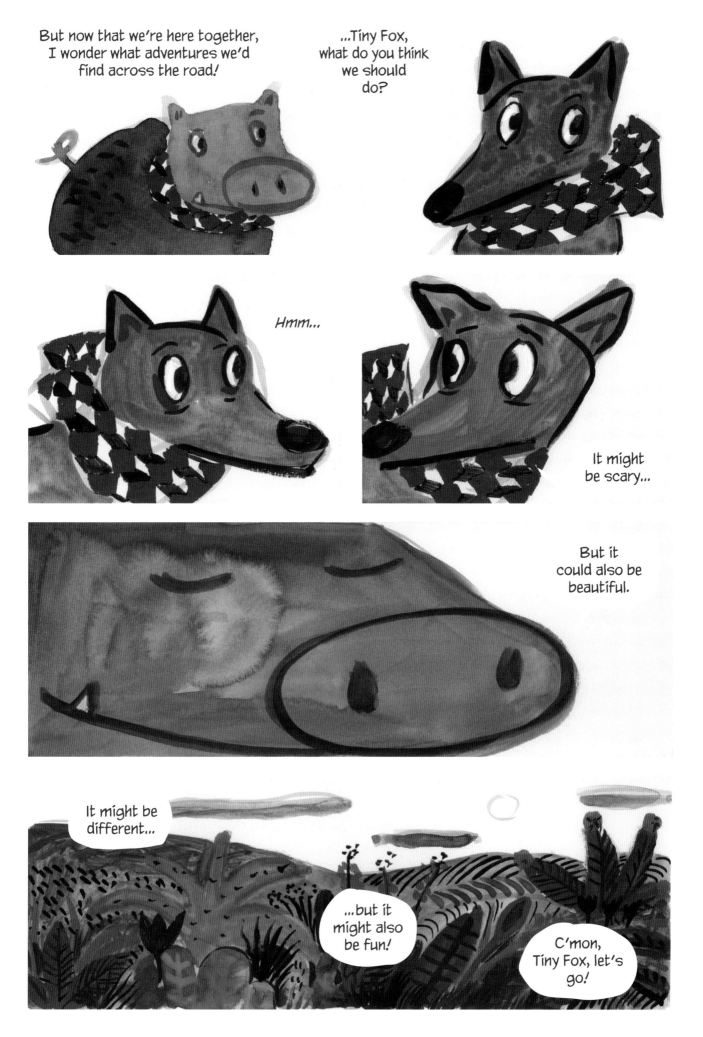

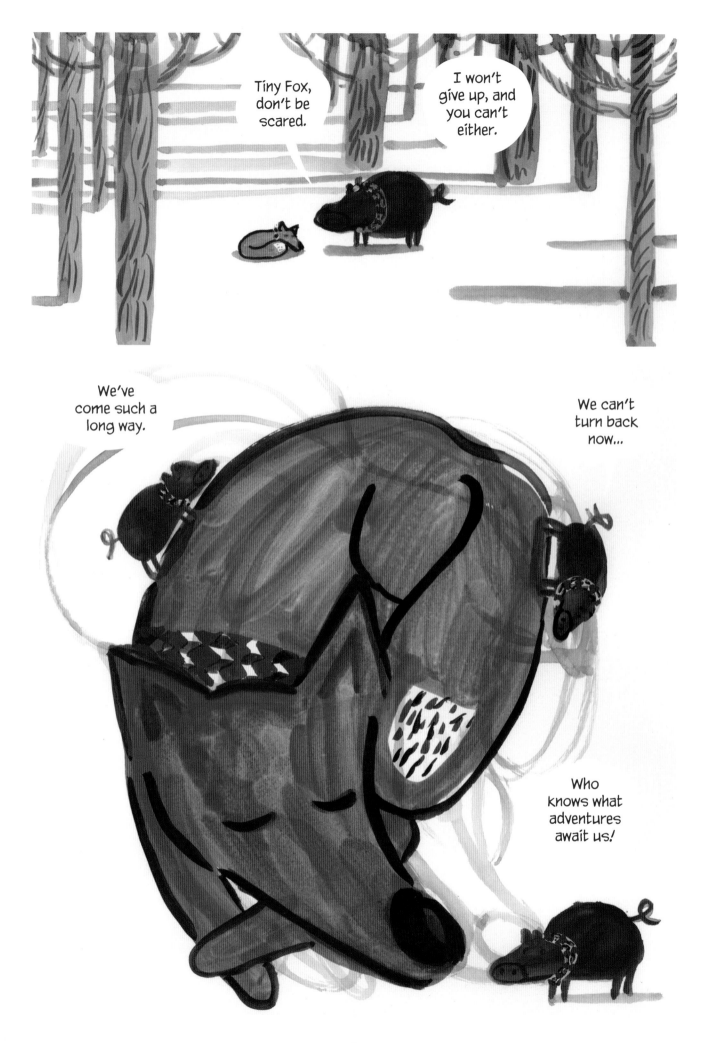

And so Tiny Fox took a deep breath and carried on, two brave friends, **together**.
Tiny Fox, look ahead! It is so beautiful and lush!
Oh, Great Boar, it's incredible! I can't believe I almost missed it!
THE END

A cover sketch for the original Polish edition of *Tiny Fox and Great Boar*.

A sketch of Tiny Fox and Great Boar. Can you tell how much they have changed from this sketch to the story you just read?

Another sketch of Tiny Fox and Great Boar.
Have you ever made a new friend unexpectedly?

Good friends stick together no matter what time of year!
What is your favorite time of year?

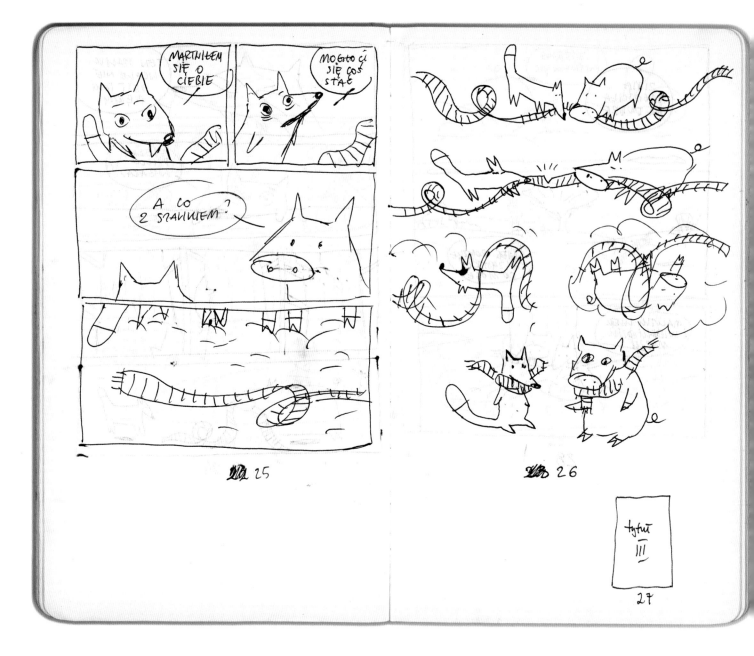

Berenika's original sketch pages of Tiny Fox and Great Boar
and the scarf they find!

Another page from Berenika's sketchbook of Tiny Fox and Great Boar
arriving at their new home.

Berenika Kołomycka

Berenika Kołomycka is a comics author, sketch artist, sculptor, and graphic artist. She graduated from the Academy of Fine Arts in Warsaw and earned the Grand Prix for comics at the International Festival of Comics and Games in Łódź. Her works have been published in both Polish and foreign magazines, as well as in schoolbooks. She regularly conducts comic workshops for adults and children. The children's series *Tiny Fox and Great Boar* is her first solo project. Outside of her work, she enjoys taking care of her cat, Mami, and her dog, Kuka.

Crank!

Christopher Crank (crank!) has lettered a bunch of books put out by Image, Dark Horse, Oni Press, Dynamite, and elsewhere. He also has a podcast with comic artist Mike Norton and members of Four Star Studios in Chicago (crankcast.com), and makes music (sonomorti.bandcamp.com). Catch him on Twitter: @ccrank and Instagram: ccrank